THIS WALKER BOOK BELONGS TO:

_____

_____

_____

_____

To Ben
C.A.

The Pocket Mouse was originally published 1969
by Hamish Hamilton Children's Books Ltd.
Published by Julia MacRae Books 1990
This edition published 1992 by Walker Books Ltd

Reprinted 1992

Text © 1967 Barbara Willard
Illustrations © 1990 Caroline Anstey

Printed and bound in Great Britain by
Severnprint Ltd, Gloucester

British Library Cataloguing in Publication Data
A catalogue record for this book is
available from the British Library.
ISBN 0-7445-2364-8

The Pocket Mouse

Barbara Willard

Illustrated by Caroline Anstey

WALKER BOOKS
LONDON

Colin kept a mouse in his pocket. He gave it cake crumbs and bits of cheese whenever he could. But since the mouse was simply a stuffed one that he had had since he was very small, it could not eat the food he gave it. So his pockets grew crumbier and messier as the days went by.

Colin had a mouse in his pocket because he was staying with his grandfather and he needed something from home to keep him company. It was the first time he had gone visiting by himself. It was also the first time he had met Miss Bagley – she looked after the house and did the cooking.

"She might not like me," Colin had said to his mother when she told him he was invited to stay a few days. He really meant he might not like Miss Bagley.

"She'll like you if you're nice to her," his mother had replied.

Colin's grandfather lived in the country. His cottage was close to the village green where they played cricket in the summer evenings.

Colin would lie in bed, with the mouse now under his pillow, listening to the clonk of the ball on the bat and the voices of the players calling to one another. Miss Bagley believed that all children should be in bed nice and early.

Miss Bagley liked things to be just so but Colin found fault with everything she did.

"Oh, *look* at all these crumbs!" she cried one bedtime, as she shook out Colin's clothes before leaving them tidy for the night. She pulled out the pocket linings and flicked the crumbs out of the window. "Boys' pockets are meant for string and things," she said.

If the mouse had been in his pocket, Colin thought, that might have gone out of the window, too. Miss Bagley had neither done nor said anything the least bit unkind so far, but Colin worried for days in case she found the mouse. He told himself she would certainly throw it away.

"I shall make it a house," he decided at last. "Then it can hide." And he went to ask his grandfather for a box.

"Better look in the cupboard under the stairs," said his grandfather.

In the dark cupboard the boxes were neatly stacked one inside the other – Colin knew at once that Miss Bagley must have arranged them like that. As he tried to find the size he wanted, he knocked the whole lot over.

"What are you up to in there?" came Miss Bagley's voice.

"Grandad said I could have a box."

"What do you want it for?"

All Miss Bagley meant was: *What size do you need?* But of course Colin decided she was being nosy and interfering. He thought he would scare her.

"For my mouse," he said. "So that it won't run about all over the place and get into people's beds."

"Oh I see," said Miss Bagley, not at all alarmed. "*That's* why you have crumbs in your pocket... We'd better find a wooden box."

"Cardboard would do."

"Oh no, Colin," Miss Bagley said. "Any mouse will gnaw its way out of a cardboard box."

Not *any* mouse, as Colin knew – but he nodded as solemnly as he could. Miss Bagley seemed to know quite a lot about mice.

"I can find you just what you need," she said. "It's in the garden shed."

Colin's grandfather was digging in the garden. He looked up as Colin and Miss Bagley went by and smiled under his large white moustache.

"Found your box?" he asked.

"Just getting it," said Colin, keeping up with Miss Bagley's fast walk.

The shed was very neat – the tools were all clean, the deck-chairs tidily stacked – there were three red towers of flower-pots and a high pile of seedboxes.

"A seedbox is too flat," said Colin.

"I wouldn't dream of using a seedbox for this job," Miss Bagley replied.

She reached up to a high shelf and brought down a wooden box. It had a lid that opened, a glass front, a wheel that went round and round...

"A proper mouse house!" Colin cried. "With a wheel to push round and round when the mouse wants to go for a run!"

"Round and round and round..." agreed Miss Bagley. "Bring it indoors and give it a clean. My nephew, John, came to stay last holidays. It was his. Now it's yours."

"Oh, *thanks!*" said Colin. And he almost smiled at her. "The fastening's broken a bit. Can I have a piece of string to mend it?"

"When my brothers were your age, they had all the string they needed in their pockets. And knives to cut it. But of course if you *will* fill up your pockets with mice and crumbs..." She was laughing at him; but he just managed not to laugh back.

Colin cleaned the house in the kitchen, mended the fastening with string from the dresser drawer, and was just tearing up newspaper for a bed when his grandfather came in from the garden.

"I didn't know you had a mouse, Colin."

Miss Bagley was peeling apples near the sink. Colin whispered to his grandfather, "It's not really real. But don't tell her."

"Not a word," he whispered back. Then he stretched and straightened his shoulders. "Ouch –

ouch – ahhh! I've been digging too long. I need a walk. Come with me, Colin."

"Where?"

"They're cutting the barley in the big field behind the church. We'll go and see how they're getting on. Put on a jacket – it's quite cool now."

Colin rushed upstairs for his anorak. The mouse house was still in his hands, but there was no time to put the stuffed mouse into its new home. He left it where it was, tucked into the pocket of his jeans.

In the big field there was a great clatter as the huge red harvester was driven round and round. Nearly all the barley was cut by now. Soon Colin found himself dashing about with the farmer's son, then wrestling and rolling in the hard stubble. He got so hot that he dragged off his anorak and flung it down by the hedge. He would have left it lying there when it was time to go home, only his grandfather sent him back for it.

"And put it on, or you'll catch cold."

Colin sighed, but did as he was told. Then he fished in the pocket of his jeans for the mouse. He dropped it carefully into the pocket of his anorak, then put in his hand to make sure it was comfortably settled.

He snatched his hand out again as though it had been bitten – as though the mouse had bitten it.

He stared at his finger. It *was* bitten! There were teeth-marks so small that they looked as though they had been made by pins.

Whatever Colin had told his grandfather about the mouse not being a real one, in his pocket at this moment there was something warm and alive and furry.

It seemed a very long time indeed from the moment when Colin had found something alive in his pocket to the moment when, alone in his bedroom, he was able to discover what it was.

At last, almost shivering with excitement, he slid his hand carefully into his pocket and brought out what was lying there.

It was the smallest mouse he had ever seen. It was so small, so delicate, that he was afraid he might hurt it just by holding it in his hands. Very cautiously he opened his fingers.

The mouse moved swiftly. Colin thought it would escape. But it only wound its long tail quickly and nervously round his finger. It sat up, paws lifted and whiskers twitching. Its bright sharp eyes were as black as the bead eyes of Colin's own stuffed mouse.

Where had it come from? It was certainly not his stuffed mouse come magically to life – for that was still in his pocket. The real mouse must have crept into the pocket of Colin's anorak as it lay on the ground in the barley field. The harvester would have left it without any place to hide, and so it had run into the pocket for safety.

"You chose the right pocket," Colin told the mouse. "You're safe now. You shall live in a house all your own."

He opened the lid of the mouse house and popped the newcomer inside. At once the mouse disappeared under the bed of torn newspaper.

"Supper!" called Miss Bagley, from the foot of the stairs.

Colin dropped the stuffed mouse in with the real one for company, slid the house under his bed and ran downstairs.

Colin had his supper on a tray in the sitting-room. His grandfather read the newspaper, and Miss Bagley sewed.

"Please may I have some cheese for my mouse?" he asked her.

"Well, see that it eats up every bit and doesn't leave crumbs in your pocket."

"No," said his grandfather. "No crumbs, Colin." And he looked over the top of his newspaper and winked.

Colin was now in a muddle. He had invented a real mouse to tease Miss Bagley, and his grandfather still thought it was all a joke.

"My nephew John's mouse liked raisins," Miss Bagley said. "But he didn't have it for long."

Colin frowned. "Why not?"

"It was a field mouse. It could only be happy in a field."

Was *his* mouse a field mouse, Colin wondered. Surely it must be.

"Is a field mouse very tiny? Has it got a windey tail?"

"No – that's a harvest mouse," his grandfather said.

Harvest meant grain and nuts and berries. Colin thought he was luckier than John had been. He would be able to make a harvest for a harvest mouse.

For once, Colin could hardly wait to get upstairs to bed. He thought Miss Bagley would never go away. She took ages to tidy up and say goodnight. The moment he was alone, he was out of bed and groping for the mouse house. He peered through the glass. There was a movement down in one corner. He saw the mouse sitting up, busily eating.

"Ohhhh!" wailed Colin.

The harvest mouse had eaten the head of the poor stuffed mouse, bead eyes, whiskers and all.

After its big meal, the harvest mouse slept. Colin slept, too. The dark night came, and then the moon rose. In the garden the trees were blue and the shadows crimson, and all the grass looked like silver matting.

It was quiet in Colin's room. Then a little sound began. It went on and on, on and on, never getting much louder. Disturbed, Colin threw himself over onto his back and began to wake up. The scratching, whirring sound went on – and on and on... Scratch, scratch... Whirr, whirr, whirr... Then Colin was wide awake and remembering the mouse.

He listened, very stiff and still in his bed. He knew what was happening. The mouse was turning the wheel up in the top corner of its house.

Where did the mouse think it was? The stillness of the night, the strangeness of the moonlight filled Colin with fears and worries. Perhaps the mouse thought it was on its way back to the barley field. But it was hurrying along a road that would never end, for it only went round and round.

At last the mouse was quiet. It had dropped down to sleep, worn out by its endless journey.

When morning came, Colin gave the mouse cheese and cake crumbs and three raisins. It sat on his hand and twisted its tail round his finger, hanging on tight.

"It doesn't even try to run away," Colin told himself. "It likes me. It likes the house. It likes going for a run on the wheel. It's a happy mouse."

All that day, Colin kept the secret. Whenever he could, he ran to his room, pulled the mouse house from under his bed and peered inside. And all that day the mouse slept. It woke up only when night came and the moon was at the window. Then it ran up into the wheel and started again on its whirring journey.

Colin tried not to hear. He stuffed his fingers into his ears. He pulled the pillow over his head. But he heard the small noise just the same. He kept thinking about John's field mouse. Why had he not asked what happened to it? It was no good trying to sleep. Colin got out of bed. He put on his slippers and dressing-gown. He looked out of the window.

The garden lay quiet and moonlit.
He could see the church and beyond it the trees by
the corner of the big field – the harvest field where
the mouse had lived.

Colin took the mouse in his hand. He stroked it and talked to it, then slipped it into his dressing-gown pocket. He opened his bedroom door and stepped out on to the landing. The clock in the hall made its deep slow *tocking*. A tap dripped in the kitchen. The tank sighed and gurgled up in the roof. Chairs creaked as they stretched after the day's work.

A door behind him opened, and he jumped so much that he almost jerked a cry out of himself.

"What's the matter?" asked Miss Bagley softly.

"What did John do with his mouse?" Colin asked.

"John? Oh-oh, of course... He took it back to the field it had come from. Why?"

"I've got to take my mouse back," said Colin. "My harvest mouse. It's no good. It doesn't like living in a box."

"Oh, Colin," said Miss Bagley, very quietly, so as not to wake his grandfather. "I thought you were teasing me. I thought it was just a pretend mouse. Didn't I see you with a stuffed mouse one day?"

"I was teasing to start with. But a real mouse got into my pocket... It can't stay in the mouse house, Miss Bagley. It thinks it can get out if it hurries, but the wheel only goes round and round."

Miss Bagley did not say *It'll do in the morning*. She said, "We'll go together, shall we? Just wait till I put on some shoes."

It was very strange indeed to be walking through the village in the deep night, not a soul to be seen, not a dog barking or a child crying, and only a cat or two enjoying the moonlight.

"I couldn't have come all this way by myself in the night-time," Colin said.

"Oh *no* – nor could I," replied Miss Bagley.

Now they were in the big stubbly field – the harvest field.

"It was just over there," said Colin. "I was playing with the others, and I left my anorak on the ground."

They went to the exact spot. Colin took the mouse from his pocket, and it stayed on his hand, its tail twining as usual round his finger. Then suddenly it seemed to know it was home. Up went its nose, its whiskers twitched wildly. One instant it was still there on his open hand – the next it had jumped and vanished utterly, so small that it was lost to sight the very second it reached the ground and the cut stalks of barley.

"There," said Miss Bagley. "Now we're all happy."

The mouse house went back into the garden shed, and all that was left of the poor stuffed mouse went into the dustbin.

"Once I had two mice," said Colin sadly, "and now I haven't got one."

Now the holiday was over, and Colin's mother came to fetch him.

"Tell me all about it," she said, as they drove off comfortably together. "Have you enjoyed yourself? Have you been good?"

But Colin was groping in his pocket and did not reply at once. Frowning with surprise, he brought out two objects and looked at them lying in his palm.

"What have you got there?" his mother asked.

"A pocket knife," he said, grinning with pleasure. "And – a pocket mouse."

It was made of twisted string, cleverly knotted together, with loops for ears and a longer tail than even a harvest mouse. He knew at once who had made it and slipped it into his pocket.

"And were you nice to Miss Bagley?" his mother asked next.

"Well, she was nice to me," said Colin.

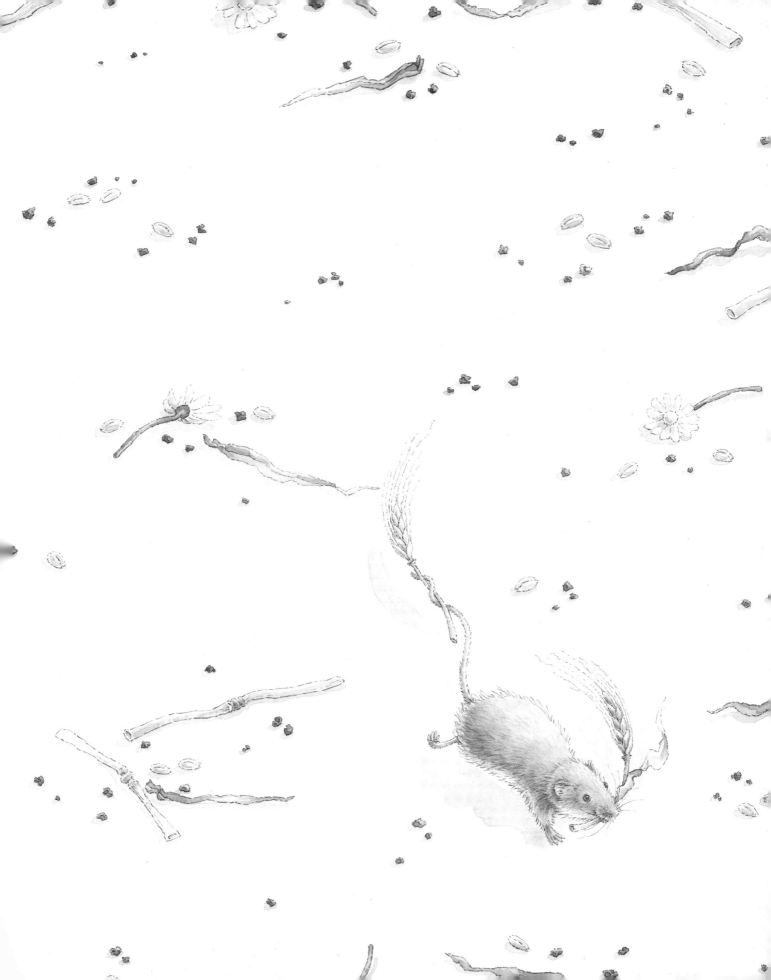

MORE WALKER PAPERBACKS
For You to Enjoy

I BOUGHT MY LOVE A TABBY CAT
by Colin West/Caroline Anstey

Have you ever seen a tabby cat in a velvet hat, or a big fat pig in a fancy wig,
or an old grey goose in dainty shoes?
These are just a few of the extraordinary guests at a wedding, where the animals
are better dressed than the bride!

"A nonsense rhyme that compares with Edward Lear at his best …
fitting and very funny illustrations." *Parents*

0-7445-2348-6   £3.99

MARY MARY
by Sarah Hayes/Helen Craig

When Mary Mary says she's not afraid of the giant who lives on the hill,
no one believes her; they just think she's being contrary as usual.
So Mary Mary sets off to visit the giant – and nothing is quite the same again!

"Helen Craig's pictures of the giant are just right." *The Teacher*

0-7445-2062-2   £3.99

THE PANTOMIME WITCH
by Hannah Cole/Dawn Aldridge

When Grandpa takes Angela and Carole to the pantomime, Angela takes her teddy Fergus too.
But at the theatre, something terrible happens
and Grandpa finds himself facing the wicked green witch!

"The story itself is very good … exceptionally good illustrations."
Recent Children's Fiction

0-7445-2363-X   £3.99

Walker Paperbacks are available from most booksellers, or by post from
Walker Books Ltd, PO Box 11, Falmouth, Cornwall TR10 9EN.

To order, send:
Title, author, ISBN number and price for each book ordered
Your full name and address
Cheque or postal order for the total amount, plus postage and packing:

UK and BFPO Customers – £1.00 for first book, plus 50p for the second book and plus 30p for each additional book to a maximum charge of £3.00.
Overseas and Eire Customers – £2.00 for first book, plus £1.00 for the second book and plus 50p per copy for each additional book.
Prices are correct at time of going to press, but are subject to change without notice.